Firstly published in 2013
by
RAGING AARDVARK PUBLISHING, Brisbane, Australia

http://ragingaardvark.com

Cover Design by Annie Evett
ISBN: 0-9875331-9-3
ISBN-13: 978-0-9875331-9-7

Twisted Tales
showcases
the winners of one of the
competitions held celebrating
(Inter) National Flash Fiction Day 2013.

CONTENT

DEDICATION

The visual image of a partying aardvark was long-time joke between my late husband and I as a symbol of all that was outrageous, impossible and left field.

I took this symbol and its essence on when Raging Aardvark Publications was created, with the vision to continue pushing the boundaries and to expect outrageous, impossible opportunities.

In particular, this anthology is dedicated to Adrian, my wonderful husband who, tragically, died this year amongst the initial editing process.

His belief in me as a writer and publisher – together with my ability to uncover gems; whether it was a quirky story, an off-kilter concept or another writer who needed a hand up – kept my passion fuelled during the dark times.

His unwavering support for me to follow my passion of encouraging and empowering writers from round the globe has been a source of strength through this difficult period.

ACKNOWLEDGEMENTS

A huge thanks to all writers who submitted to the competition celebrating the second (Inter)National Flash Fiction Day. It was wonderful to include established writers beside emerging authors and heart-warming to receive emails from thrilled contributors excited to launch their careers within this anthology. The support and encouragement this project receives was so much appreciated.

Thank you to Ether Books, in particular Chris who works as their Content Creator; for all his valued assistance in the selection process.

Without the support and encouragement of Calum Kerr, Director of (Inter)National Flash Fiction Day, this collection would not have reached the audiences and garnered the interest it has.

To the wonderful writers, and fellow editors who have offered their support and understanding to me during tragic times which prevented this anthology to be published in its normal timely manner – a huge debt of gratitude.

Most importantly, I'd like to thank my long suffering family and close friends for their ongoing support and encouragement. Twisted Tales, and all of the creations within Raging Aardvark Publishing, would truly not happen without them.

Annie Evett
Publisher

Foreword

Welcome to the second edition of Twisted Tales, an anthology celebrating Flash Fiction in its own right.

Short, sweet snippets of stories which have the ability to tempt the imagination, tantalise a reader and pose questions form the heart of a great flash fiction. Twisted Tales was born out of the need to showcase flash fiction in its own right and a desire to present writers whose first love lies within the short story.

It's heartening to see the gradual wave of acceptance within the reading and publishing communities for the various formats of the short story.

This collection investigates the thin line between the good in us all, and the lurking evil. Some of the stories seek the motivation, others deliberately take an opposing view, but all will surprise you with their perspective.

The collection was first published in digital form on the mobile social media platform, Ether Books as part of the celebrations of Flash Fiction Day. It is also available as an e-book with the blessings of all involved to share and enjoy the work held within.

Annie Evett
Editor

Once again Annie's given me the honour of assisting her with the editing of Twisted Tales for 2013. Such a buzz!

This year's crop of stories is as wonderful as last year's. Imagine being a judge - what a difficult job!

I don't have a 'favourite'; I enjoyed reading all of the contributions and marvel at how we, as writers, keep coming up with variations on the seven story archetypes.

Keep on keeping on and I so look forward to assisting with next year's editing (please, Annie).

Margie Riley
Editor

American Cream

by Melissa Gutierrez

We made Jill a milkshake made of glue. Terry dared us. We wanted to know a couple of things: if it was possible to make a glue milkshake at all, whether someone drinking it could tell the difference, and what would happen to the drinker once he or she drank. I mean, we all wanted to know all this, but it was Terry who had dared us to pick Jill.

Jill was the perfect candidate. She wasn't too skinny to refuse a milkshake, nor too fat to be called a bully's easy target if the prank got caught. She was medium and all too nice—so sweet and grateful when we asked her if she'd like a milkshake that we almost felt a little guilty. Okay, we definitely did.

We had to really stage the act, you know, couldn't just invite her over for a milkshake while the rest of us just watched and grinned. So we perfected up the glueshake mix a whole week in advance, all of us taking turns taste-testing and then spitting out on the kitchen floor, the walls, each other. You know—boys. The final version involved a lot of artificial sweetener, vanilla extract, corn starch, and—get this—a little bit of oil to keep everything from sticking. At first we had trouble with the glue freezing and quickly learned to mix it with hot milk first, then put it in the fridge to set, then fold it in the blended ice cream mix. It ended up being pretty good. We would have maybe drunk it all ourselves, if we hadn't set on Jill.

When we had her over, we made a batch of vanilla shakes right there before her very eyes, then had this whole scheme all set up to distract her while we switched one of the regular milkshakes for the glueshake in the fridge: Terry would moon her. He would say "Hey Jill," and drop his pants, and she would either stare and stare or close her eyes—and either way the plan was foolproof. It worked, of course, but it got weird when she stood up just behind him and put one of her soft hands on each his cheeks.

Well, that really messed things up. We all got hardons instantly, and everybody dropped their jaws. We stopped what we were doing in the kitchen and just stared in shock and disbelief.

To this day I am not sure—no one is, even after much debate—where the glueshake actually ended up. Because then what happened was that Jill did this: she pet his arse. Not even squeezed or rubbed. But pet. Just once or twice or maybe three times, even—we should know, the way we were all watching, or maybe we shouldn't, maybe we were just too dazed. And then she just said, "Okay," and sat back down. Terry pulled his pants up pretty slow, like, should I, guys? Are we done here or did the plan change now or what? Lyle nodded at him, just nodded, and we were all like, nodding what? Nodding like the glueshake is in position, or nodding like, I don't know what the hell just happened either? And when Terry clicked his belt back on we all snapped back to earth. Lyle brought the tray of milkshakes out and we all jumped to take the ones around the edge, like planned, even though we weren't so sure.

Jill took the center one like she was supposed to, and then she said, "To Terry's butt."

"To Terry's butt," we said, and clinked our plastic glasses. Then everybody took a sip—we all eyed each other over cup rims, but Jill drank with her eyes closed, like everything was bliss.

Wind Chimes

by Penegrin Shaw

Wind chimes. How I hate them. How you must hate them; this constant percussion polluting an otherwise peaceful place. It is wrong, unholy even, tacky.

I have a cloth with me as I always do; all purpose, blue, daisy cloth. I use it to wipe your headstone, removing the grass from the caretaker's lawnmower, watermarks from acid rain.

Moss, mould and algae, it always returns.

I wipe marks from your face, set in the stone in colour, taken from an old photograph when you were smiling.

Birds watch me do all this. The jackdaw nods approval.

I miss you. I come here the most. It says a lot, speaks volumes, under the wind chimes.

I remove the old rotting flower stems; empty the brown water, clean it, refill it at the tap at the end of your row.

I open the bouquet and lay the flowers in the paper they were wrapped in. I cut off the bottoms of the stems with scissors that I brought with me and vary the heights of the flowers.

I never buy a bouquet that is made. I go custom. I choose each flower. I pick each one for you; colours and shapes that you would approve of.

I miss you. A tear meets the marble above where you lie in the earth, my gift. No hand reaches up to take it and I wipe it with the daisy cloth, in case it leads to more growth or fungus upon your stone. It bothers me that your shrine is under attack from the elements and one day I won't be here to make it look nice, to honour you.

The time we spent together, I miss it. I miss your smell, not the perfume you wore, the scent beneath it, you in the morning lying next to me.

Sex is missed too, I must admit this; the sweat, the writhing, weaving two into one tapestry.

People say you move on. You grieve–you speak to people about it. Repair. Find someone new. I'm not sure I will ever find another like you; the perfect mix of innocence and cheekiness, a single dimple when you smiled.

The flowers look perfect. I didn't know I had such talent. You didn't know.

Kneeling on the grass, I picture you below me, encased in walnut with blue silk inner lining.

Are you being devoured by insects or animal? Are you skull and bone with exposed rib cage under your dress? Has your red hair fallen free from your scalp?

An elderly lady walks by and gives me a nod of approval for being here, an air of sadness about that nod. I send a nod back to her in the same way and she leaves.

I must go now, but I will be back my dear, soon.

Before I go, I want to tell you that I put you there because this is what I do. I come here because I enjoy celebrating your death at my hands. I met your parents here once and we cried together.
I chose you that night because of your single, prominent, dimple and I killed you for it. Then I enjoyed you in other ways. Wind chimes. I hate them, but I will leave them swinging in the trees, because I imagine you hate them too.

I will be back soon my dear and I will bring you flowers when these pretty ones have died too, like the others.

Hum

by Lance Manion

A wise man once told me that a ladder is not an upside down hole ... so you can see why I am leery of advice. He really was a wise man but I can't help thinking that on that particular day he was a bit off his game. He might have even been the man who started me on the whole "either/or" game that has been part of my life since I was little.

It started innocently enough. If I dropped my ice cream I would think to myself that I would rather have dropped it than maintained control and been hit by a car an hour later. Using this little ploy I always felt that things turned out for the best. As I got older this very simplistic way of looking at things continued. Anything bad that happened was immediately made better by the idea that something much worse could have happened had the original bad thing not transpired. I was never going to win the lottery but I was also sure that I would never contract some deadly rotting disease and this made my very ordinary life seem O.K.

I was O.K. with things.

Except love.

I remained jealous of those lucky bastards who had experienced true love. I didn't envy getting laid or dating or marriage. Nope. Not in the least. I envied those moments I saw played out so very infrequently where it was obvious to everyone involved that the two people on the main stage were in the midst of it. Sometimes it was a kiss and sometimes it was slap or a raised voice but it would resonate with everyone as if someone had flicked a tuning fork.

It would hum.

I had never hummed.

Until five minutes ago when she walked in.

I was working as a busboy and she walked in and although I was still a busboy doing busboy things I was really something more. She was a human sparkler and as she walked little bits of light popped and hissed and tumbled to the ground around her and I was sure I was the only one who saw it and if I could only tell her about it she would recognise me as someone special in her life and we could begin whatever it was we seemed destined to begin.

Instead she pulled a gun and hurried all of us in the restaurant into the back room as her friend cleaned out the cash register. By all of us I should say me, the waitress and the cook. It wasn't a very big restaurant. She tied up Betsy and Paul but stuck me in the walk-in freezer as I followed my instincts and began to explain in greater-than-necessary detail how she sparkled.

She was having none of it.

I looked out through the little round window set in the large iron door, like the kind they have in airplane doors I guess is the best way to explain it, and saw her take one more look in my direction before she turned and departed. At that moment I put my hand against the glass like I'd seen done in so many romantic movies and sobbed. The hand pressed against the glass. Fingers spread like a frozen wave goodbye.

Classic.

A sob like a hum.

A hum I wouldn't have traded for not getting hit by a car or getting the worst rotting disease you can think up or even not getting trapped in a meat locker with nobody in any position to let me out and my core temperature plummeting quickly.

Or even not having her come back a few minutes later and kill both Betsy and Paul with quick shots to the head before letting me out and asking if I really thought she sparkled.

These Dark Enemies
by Kenneth Crowther

Alone.

No backup.

Who would I call anyway? No one comes to my aid at the best of times. And this is far from one of my best times.

I consider calling out and decide against it. I'm not sure if I want anyone to know. To be honest, I'm not really sure of anything. High strung emotional claustrophobia is pouring a thick fog into my brain, muddling my mind.

I can't believe I'm here again. It feels like every day.

Sometimes more, sometimes less. But it's becoming unbearable. So alone. An overwhelming stale clinical whiteness floods my eyes, so I close them. What is it that Peter Pan says, think happy thoughts? I bet he was never in my situation. Things like this don't happen in Never-Never Land. Captain Hook is nothing compared to my demons.

How can I think happy thoughts when the pain is so intense? It tears through my consciousness and my mind swims. Sad thoughts! Sad thoughts!

The enemy is large. They're stronger than usual and

I can feel the weight of it pressing upon me.

Stabs of pain erupt through my body as ever so slowly they torture me, cutting me in half.

Must. Get. Through. This.

I grit my teeth and focus. I try to push the pain from my mind. How did it come to this? It wasn't that long ago that I was sitting at my desk working at the McKlinsky file. Damn McKlinsky. Could this be his fault? Was I so engrossed in his deductibles that I didn't notice their approach?

They came while I sat. Before I knew what was happening they were upon me. These dark enemies. They grabbed me roughly and jerked me upright. I reached out for the keyboard earnestly and closed McKlinsky's file. Client privacy. One of them punched me in the gut and I doubled over, all air leaving me at once. From my bent position my eyes searched the room for help.

Nothing. The room was full of people, but no one had noticed! How could they not? Could they not see what was happening before their eyes? Were they ignoring me? Or were they so obsessed with their own McKlinskys that they were simply oblivious? Or maybe. God – the thought rocked me – maybe they were in on it.

Can't ask for help. They won't help.

I was hauled from my cubicle and my sight grew dim. The pain was spreading. Fumbling through the corridors I felt my assailants lead me out of the main office building and through a series of doors.

And then, here I am.

They are with me. They torture me for answers. I know what they want. I want to give it up!

Don't you see! I want to help you, but I can't. I would if I could, honestly, please believe me. They push harder and I cry out in agony, shutting my mouth quickly and praying to a God I don't believe in that no one heard.

I will not break. Deep breath. I will not break!

Sweat. Tears... Hopefully no blood.

And then it happens – release. Sweet, glorious, holy release.

The longest exhale of my life and a weak smile creases upon my face. It's over. They're gone.

The small room radiates my joy. All at once I feel freed. Pain lingers for a few moments longer and then dissipates completely. I lean back and take one more deep breath. I reach for the paper and my breath catches again as my fingers meet the depleted cardboard roll mounted on the wall.

Bloody hell.

I look between my legs. These dark enemies luxuriate in tepid water, gently bobbing up and down. Grinning evil grins. Their torment continues.

I consider calling for help.

Vanilla and Caramel

by Kate Murray

A special messenger brought a sealed envelope to the house with a sheet of paper inside bearing Maria's delicate hand. I couldn't believe what I saw.

"Oops!"

My voice echoed around the silent kitchen. Really it wasn't my fault. If she had told me then things would be different, but she hadn't.

I remember the first time I saw her hair lit from the sun.

She had looked like a goddess, all golds and reds. I really loved her hair, beautiful burnt orange with a natural wave. When the light shone through it rubies would glisten and sparkle. I'd been surprised when I'd found out it was her natural colour. Sure, there'd been a couple of greys sneaking in but I'd managed to persuade her not to cover them up. I told her they heightened her beauty by showing she'd lived, and she'd fallen for it. I just don't like the chemical smell that comes with dyes.

No, I prefer my women natural so that I can truly detect their natural smell, their perfume. Maria was a delectable mix of vanilla and caramel, so good I could bury myself in her scent for hours at a time.

Placing the letter to my nose I inhale, vanilla and caramel. Delightful. I was going to miss her.

Looking down I read the note again. Apparently her mother was ill and she would be gone for a couple of days but be back for Christmas. She even apologised for writing the letter as she knew I would be at work, so she was having it delivered especially for when I was home. There were even some home-baked vanilla and caramel cookies in the tin.

Honestly, she never mentioned any of this.

I'd walked in on her packing.

"What are you doing?" I'd asked, keeping my voice calm and even. She'd seemed startled and had turned to me with a pink top in her hands. Odd that, I remember the top with its cream detailing. It was one of my favourites and I gestured to it as I asked the quiet question.

"To remember you," she said and smiled. Perhaps if she hadn't smiled... But she did and I got so angry. I thought she was leaving me. I snatched the top away and tore it down the middle.

To tell you the truth I was as shocked as she was that it ripped. But then these clothes made in China are not robust. She just stood there with her beautiful hair framing her face; all pale and shocked. Even in my anger I desired her.

"You're leaving me?" I screamed and she winced as if I'd struck her, which is what I did. Not a slap but a right hook. She never looked away from my eyes so she never saw it coming. Just as my fist cracked her cheekbone she'd muttered something. At the time I'd dismissed it but I think she may have said something like 'letter'. As I mentioned earlier – oops.

Of course she hit the floor totally insensible. Then, well I'm a little ashamed to say I lost track of my actions. Let's just say that we ended up in the cellar and, looking at this letter I think I need to apologise.

Holding the letter to my nose I breathe in her scent again and walk down the stairs and into the cool dampness. The first thing I see is her hair floating as if in a breeze. I kneel and bring myself in direct eye-line with the orange beauty.

"Honey, I'm sorry." She doesn't respond. Sighing, I grab some cello-tape from the desk behind me and turn to my vanilla and caramel. Gently and oh so carefully I pick up her jar and place it on the shelf, taping her letter to the lid.

"You see, sweetie, this will remind me not to lose my temper." Shaking my head at the loss, I head upstairs to start grieving. As I do I bump the shelving unit accidentally. Twelve jars shake and in each one hair waves in quietly radiant splendour. I must be more careful, I must take care of all my girls.

When Pigs Fly!

by CM Stewart

My hometown of Buell was once a dull, conservative town. Serious people having a serious time at work and at play, and going to church on Sundays. But all that changed when LabCorp moved in.

Ft. Smith put out a press release to the county of Sebastian:

LabCorp of Ft. Smith is proud to announce the successful trials of a new trans-species hybrid.

We will reveal the specifics of the hybrid next month at our community appreciation ceremony.

Exact date and time to be announced.

Buell was all abuzz. The whole town was speculating just what freak of nature LabCorp came up with. A couple people thought it might be some kind of pig-bird, as pigs and birds are pretty much the only animals in Sebastian county, except for the dogs and cats, and those creatures are, for the most part, peoples' pets. And people wouldn't take too kindly to have their pets hybridized, at least not in Sebastian County. But come on now, a pig-bird? That would mean pigs could now fly, and of course there's no crazier thought than a flying pig, as most of us agreed. And that put an end to the speculation.

But the pig-bird seed had been planted.

The town librarian, Jenny Lind, was the first to act peculiarly. When old man Grover made yet another pass at young Miss Lind, instead of turning up her nose and giving a dismissive sniff, as she'd done for the past two years, she got a twinkle in her eye and a smirk on her lips. She said, "Grover, I'll let you kiss me when pigs fly! In fact, I'll even kiss you myself when pigs fly!" She said that on duty in the Buell Library, right there at the front desk. Now, not many Buellians heard, as not many Buellians visit the library, but gossip spreads fast in a small town like Buell.

The very next night, Rocky Biggs, the town's bar bouncer, said, "I'll wear a purple tutu when pigs fly!" He said that in front of everybody (it was Saturday night at the Buell Bar and Grill). It got a big laugh, and soon everybody in the bar was saying what they would do when pigs flew.

Some said they would dance in the street. Some said they would stop going to church, even on Christmas and Easter. And some even said they would go skinny-dipping in the daytime! Of course, we knew there could never be any such thing as a flying pig, not even out of LabCorp, and so we didn't really expect to have to act on our words.

The following Monday, Whitey Bluff, the town administrator, took it upon himself to hop on his motor scooter and go up to Ft. Smith. He said he was going take a look at the hybrid animals, in an official capacity, as administrator of Buell.

We didn't hear from him for nearly a week. He didn't even answer his cell phone. We Buellians knew it wasn't like Whitey to abandon his administrative duties. So we went to church and prayed and kept vigil. And when Whitey finally came riding back down the main street of Buell on his motor scooter with a shoebox strapped to the back, we could barely restrain ourselves.

Whitey called a town meeting. When all were present and accounted for, we gathered round, and he opened the shoe box. Inside were five little piglet-fledglings, all pink and squeaking. Real live baby pig-birds.

Jenny Lind grabbed old man Grover and kissed him full on the lips in front of everybody. That night Rocky Biggs showed up for work at the bar and grill wearing a purple tutu. People danced in the street. They stopped going to church. Some of them even skinny dipped in the daytime, just like they said they would!

We all took turns feeding the little pig-birds worms and grubs. We forgot all about LabCorp's community appreciation ceremony. After a while, the pig-birds grew feathers and flew away.

They were tiny little things, with wings and beaks and claws. Probably only two percent pig. But they were pig-birds alright. They really did fly.

Woman's Best Friend

by Cathy Lennon

In a snoring competition it would be a dead heat between him and the dog. Though dog at least is on the floor. When jabbed, dog takes it in good part; acceptance following surprise.

Husband on the other hand, does not. He growls. Next time, I'll aim for the throat.

We are great gourmands, dog and I. The kitchen, our domain, is larded with aromas that have us salivating. Eyes bright, we tremble and lick our lips, lunging for stray morsels, scrounging every last drop with concentration. "I wish they'd invent a pill," husband sighs, when I ask what he would like for dinner. Dog's eyebrows flick and we exchange a look.

"Come to the beach!" I say, longing for endless sky and the edge of things. He wrinkles his nose and reaches for the TV remote. Dog and I roam over clean-washed sands, free and buffeted by ozone winds. We close our eyes and face the horizon, scent the rhythmic waves, our mouths wide with joy.

When the letter came, confirming the bad thing I knew, I left it on the table. He gave my shoulder a pat, fair enough. But it was dog who got me through. The quiet company in my grief, the sympathetic gaze, the tender head laid in my lap.

Before the log stove we laze, bellies soft under caressing hands. Hot fur and no expectation.

His deep brown eyes observe, his lips fall back to reveal teeth that could kill but we trust each other, dog and I. Reluctantly I go upstairs to claim my allotted inches of bed. I lie balanced on one hip. These shoulder blades could slice him in half, but still the hand comes over. In the darkness I bare my fangs and suppress a snarl.

They say that animals are dumb. I don't agree. Yackety-yack on his mobile phone. 'Mate' this and 'Cheers' that.

Dog retires upstairs, leaving this to me. I reach past him to open the door. He frowns, the conversation ongoing, and I push him outside. His lips are moving still, I can see him through the window. I open the casement and throw him a collar and lead. "Go away!" I shout. "Shoo!"

In our room, dog stretches out on the bed. I let him.

Clown

by Jacqueline Pye

The word that means a fear of clowns is 'coulrophobia'.

I know this because I read it in a book given to me last year for my eighth birthday and it made me feel sick. I never liked clowns, ever since we were at the circus when I was five, and one pretended to throw a bucket of water over me when it was only pieces of paper. They are The Enemy now.

When I'm being naughty, my brother Jack says, "Don't be such a clown", because he knows I don't like that at all.

Jack was excited when he heard the circus was coming. He wanted to go – begged, and saved up the money from his paper round. Dad eventually agreed – I think he was always going to anyway.

I really, really didn't want to go, but Dad said I had to.

We arrived early, and some pretty weird people were wandering around in horrid outfits, chatting to children.

"I wish I was somewhere else."

Jack gave me a push and said, "Don't be a misery."

At least there were a few fairground stalls. I wanted

to try for a huge stuffed giraffe, but Dad said no-one ever wins those. Then, out of the corner of my eye I caught sight of someone standing close by. A clown, and he was looking in my direction. Watching me. Whitened eyes with a black cross over each, a round red nose, and a painted on smile although he wasn't actually smiling.

I asked Dad for money for a burger, and slipped away to escape from The Enemy. As I paid and took my burger, a hand on my shoulder made me jump.

"Hello. I saw you looking at the giraffe. You liked him, I could tell."

"Yes, I did. But now I have to get back to my Dad."

"I won a giraffe earlier, but I don't really want him. Would you like him?"

My instinct was to run – I couldn't see Dad and Jack but I knew roughly where they'd be. But with all the people around, there didn't seem to be much stranger danger and I did like the giraffe. So I followed.

At a grubby little caravan the clown stopped and opened the door.

"Come on in. You'll just love him. Look, there he is."

And there he was, a beautiful giraffe, nearly as tall as me, with long eyelashes. I put my hand out to stroke his furry neck, and the clown took hold of my fingers. I pulled my hand away and he closed the caravan door.

"Don't rush away, dear. Won't you tell me your name?"

"I'm not allowed."

"But it's very rude not to answer."

My heart was pounding by now. I looked around desperately and saw a long knife within reach on the drainer, next to some dirty cups and plates.

"I'll tell you if you turn away. I'm shy about things like that."

The clown chuckled. "How sweet," he said, and turned.

The next moment he cried out, and then there was blood surging from his back and all over my hands. Luckily not my blue dress or my new white shoes, just my hands. Now he was on the floor, making a strange gurgling noise, and once he went quiet I washed myself clean. His make-up was on the table, and I picked out the fat red lipstick, wiped the 'smile' from his face with his dishcloth and drew a sad mouth in its place. Then I stepped over him and let myself out into the sunshine.

"Attention please. A young girl has gone missing. She's wearing a blue dress and white shoes."

I found my way back before anyone recognised me, and Dad hugged me while Jack muttered, "Glad you're OK and everything."

Dad said I'd been naughty to be so long, but I wasn't bothered. I'd got my own back on The Enemy once and for all, and felt certain they wouldn't come after me again. Actually, I quite enjoyed that circus.

Hairdresser

by Clarissa Angus

Cecilia hasn't washed or moisturised her hands. They smell of oranges mixed with damp. Her fingertips feel like sandpaper against my face. She's in a good mood today, doesn't stop talking, her mouth unable to keep up with the thoughts tumbling out of her mind. Her hands are on rewind – they yank my hair and the whole of my scalp protests.

This is agony. I want to scream: Stop! Instead, I say, "Make me beautiful, today." It just slipped out, a reflex. It's our private joke.

Cecilia claps her hands in delight. She kisses me on the cheek. Inappropriate? Yes, but it's her way and I've come to accept it. She yells she'll be right back and leaves.

I bask in the silence. The dresser is directly in front of me, the mirror large and ornate; a 1920s Hollywood starlet's wet dream. I review my reflection and find myself appreciating how the years have been good to me as Cecilia's top client. Except for a few lost hairs (which fell out naturally) and a couple of bad makeover jobs, I'm still the type of woman most girls aspire to be: good posture, an hourglass figure, fabulous skin. I love my smile. It's the smile of a model, with eternal perfect white teeth.

Cecilia returns with a perfume bottle. She sprays

90% of its contents into my hair. She runs her fingers through it, not roughly this time. She laughs with delight. She drools.

Her fingers absently catch my string again: "Make me beautiful", I coo. I mean it this time.

Mrs Cecilia appears at her daughter's bedroom door. "Time for bed, darling."

I'm changed into a pair of pyjamas that match hers. I'm placed beside her in bed and turned onto my side so that I get a close up of her big, smiling face. I watch it until she falls asleep and think to myself that things could be worse – I could be a nappy.

The New Dress

by J Adamthwaite

Let me show you my outfit, Mum said eagerly.

It was giving her a new lease of life, all this planning. She'd been at it ever since the diagnosis.

I followed her upstairs, stopping midway for her to catch her breath, hand firmly gripping the banister. Her hair was thinning. It was the first time I'd noticed it through the tight grey curls.

There, she said, beaming, gesturing at the black sequinned dress that hung on the wardrobe door. I thought maybe I'd have a red scarf with it. What do you think?

I shrugged. What was I supposed to think? You'll look lovely, I said.

I know I'll lose weight, she said. So I bought it a size smaller.

I stared at the dress.

Cup of tea? she asked, shuffling out of the bedroom.

Her kitchen was – always had been – spotless. Everything in its place and a place for everything, she liked to say. I sat at the table and watched her squoosh teabags in bone china mugs.

Let's have a biscuit, she said, waving her hand at the tin on the table. The biscuit tin was a wedding present. It had a gold handle like a doorknob on the lid and pictures of fruit painted round the barrel. Dad tried to count the apples once when he was high on morphine. He got distressed because he couldn't remember where he'd started. She told him there were 27 and took him to bed. We know cancer well in this house.

There you are, love, she said, setting a mug in front of me and pushing the biscuit tin across the table. I stirred a sugar cube into my tea. She used to tut at sweet tea. When did she stop doing that?

You like the dress then? she asked suddenly, half way through a custard cream. It's not too dressy?

It's fine, I said.

She looked at me sternly. You'll remember which one it is?

I nodded.

She looked satisfied.

I was thinking I might look into ordering the coffin as well, she said. Save you a bit of trouble, won't it? Anyway, it'll be nice to see what I'm going in.

She took a long sip of tea.

I watched her silently as the afternoon shadows trickled across the kitchen floor.

Sarah

by Mike Epifani

I stared at my sister's porcelain doll for two hours. The glow of my sister's nightlight gave us just enough illumination to see each other. I did it while my sister slept. I sat in her plastic blue chair and stared at her doll while she breathed in the background. My sister named the doll Sarah. I liked Sarah a lot.

Sarah stared back at me with her lifeless eyes and I think she winked at me. At least I hope she did. My sister woke up and saw me sitting there and screamed. My parents came in and I had nothing to say, so I said nothing. They made me go back to my room and I dreamed of the doll's face shattering. In the dream, I smashed Sarah's face with a hammer. There was nothing but blackness, no texture, no sense of place. There was a light shining on her but it avoided me and when her face separated to my satisfaction I began to eat the pieces. They tasted like communion bread. I woke up and my jockies were wet. I changed them before going downstairs.

At school, I saw a girl that looked like Sarah. I smiled at her but she didn't smile back. I kept staring and smiling and she kept nervously glancing over. I thought she liked me but during lunch Joe told me that if I didn't stop staring at his girlfriend that he was going to hurt me. I said nothing because I had nothing to say. I wished she was more like Sarah.

On my walk home from school I found a dead squirrel. It looked at me like Sarah does. I held it in my hands and some girls from school saw me doing it. They were disgusted. I wanted to taste the squirrel but I set it back down instead. For the rest of the walk, I imagined Sarah and the squirrel and me living in a tree together. We would eat each other and have sex with each other. I like dead things. I like the way they look at me.

Later that night, once everyone was asleep, I snuck back into my sister's room to spend time with Sarah. We stared at each other for two hours and suddenly I felt an uncontrollable urge to kiss her. I knew she felt it, too. I crept over to her and we slowly kissed but maintained eye contact. My lips were doing all the work, but I could tell she liked it. I dreamed of smashing the girl from school. In the dream, her face was porcelain and fell away in pieces like Sarah's. She tasted like snickerdoodle. I woke up and had to change my jockies.

At school that day I was running late to class and the hallways were empty. The girl who looked like Sarah went into the girl's bathroom just ahead of me and I quietly followed her inside. She was in a stall and I could hear her peeing. I waited for her to finish and when she came out I covered her mouth before she could scream. I wrestled her to the tile of the bathroom floor and smashed her face against the linoleum. After eight solid cracks she stopped struggling and there as a puddle of blood. Her eyes stayed open and she stared at me, and she looked just like Sarah.

We slowly kissed but maintained eye contact.

I took out my pocket knife and cut a square out of her cheek and tasted it. It tasted like vanilla cake. I went in for seconds, then thirds, and the next thing I knew her face was skinned. She no longer looked like Sarah, but their eyes were still the same, and that was all that mattered. I cupped the side of her face.

This is what love is.

I knew I would find it.

The Secret Remains
by Donna Schwender

I started collecting secrets when I was just seven years old. Bona fide skeletons that I buried in the dusty recesses of my closet.

It all began with Peaches, the neighbours' kitten who had the juice squeezed right out of her when a FedEx delivery truck backed over her. As I watched the snow absorb the implosion of her tiny body, the driver simply continued along his own predestined route.

Instead of stealing the Christmas packages from the Samsons' garland-draped porch, the treasure that captured my attention that day was the lifeless, furry carcass that was unlike any present I'd ever received. My juvenile error was in immediately enshrining sweet Peaches in a shoebox that I lovingly placed under my bed. It had seemed like the perfect spot—there under the many watchful eyes of my Cat in the Hat bedspread—but I quickly learned that the smell of death can escape from under even the thickest blanket. I was also educated to the fact that death can get a lot juicier than one might expect.

For once, I was grateful for my mother's nicotine addiction. It had long-ago destroyed any bloodhound sniffing capabilities she might have once had. While she was locked away in her bedroom—drowning her sorrow in thick smoke and watered-down whiskey—I moved the rotting, cardboard casket to the cobweb-infested shed in our backyard. Spiders would be the only lock I needed to keep my mother from discovering my secret.

I checked on dear Peaches almost every day. No food, water, or litter box cleaning was required. Just a quick peek to see if she was ready to spend the next stage of her life sharing closet space tucked behind my toy box.

As winter slowly melted away, so too did Peaches' flesh.

Although decades of other seasons have now come and gone, I still remember the day I was finally able to pet her bones. Unfortunately, many had been shattered by the fatal impact. The hours slipped joyfully away as I tried to puzzle together what the remaining intact ones had been. Ribs and teeth were the easiest for me to identify.

After wiping away any residual scraps of life, I swaddled the skin-free pile of bones into an old sock that I'd stolen from my mother's stash of seldom-used cleaning rags. I was delighted to discover that the miniature skull of a kitten fit perfectly into the heel of it. Tying a knot at the end of the slightly holey shroud, I tucked Peaches into the pocket of my favourite pink jacket.

Before I laid her to rest in peace in my closet, I wanted her to enjoy one more sun-filled day playing outside. A bike ride around the neighbourhood ended prematurely though when Gideon, the

Samsons' Gordon Setter, insisted upon leaving snotty nose prints on my coat. Did he actually recognise the smell of his missing friend?

As Peaches and I flew high into the sky on the tire swing that my father had hung for me right before he too turned into a pile of bones, I smiled and wondered if I'd recognise the scent of him, were we lucky enough to one day meet again. My father now knew the answer to that secret, but he wasn't talking.

Third Party

by Oonah V Joslin

"Where's the party?"

It didn't look like much. Just deadbeats sitting around drinking water.

"It's a new concept in parties. An A.R. event. Alternate Reality. You've never taken squARes?" said Jas.

Trudy felt foolish. "No."

"You think of what you want, take a squARe and it alters the reality around you." She handed Trudy a sheet of coloured rice paper marked out by perforations. "Now think what kind of party you want. Elegant, fancy dress?"

"Elegant," said Trudy.

"Now put a squARe on your tongue. Go on. I use them every day."

As the paper dissolved Trudy found herself in a stunning room with chandeliers, a grand piano, other people dotted around the room.

"What a gorgeous gown, Jas. Where did you get it?"

"You can have anything you want – remember? Champagne?"

Trudy imagined herself in a full length, feathered flamingo coloured, strappy dress with a sequinned bodice, soft leather peach sandals and a saffron bag encrusted with coral beads. A few flamingo feathers adorned her honey hair. Soft music played. She conjured up an attractive date who danced sublimely.

She'd joined the others sitting around the walls drinking water and eating little bits of pastel rice paper and it was the best party she'd ever been to.

From then on Trudy kept squARes underneath papers in the locked drawer of her work station. It was handy on days when she couldn't wait to break for lunch or didn't want to see the boss, Randal Handley. He had been exceptionally friendly toward her recently even though her desk was piled high with unfinished work. Today she would avoid him. She slipped a couple of squARes into her bag and headed for the door.

La Tapas was her preferred lunchtime escape. Of course it was really just the tea shop. She ordered a 'selectione' and a glass of Rioja. Juan, her favourite waiter, had a tight butt struggling in tighter trousers. Flamenco guitars played and everything was just right.

"Ah, Miss Timpson."

Trudy coughed up a prawn. "Mr Handley! What are you doing here?"

"Having lunch," he said loudly, then in a lowered

voice, "with you Trudy. I can call you Trudy now we're not in work."

He slid onto the seat opposite her and their knees touched. She wanted to vomit.

"Did we arrange lunch?"

"Come, now Trudy. Don't go all coy on me. Tuesday's our day," his hand was creeping over her knee and upwards.

"Really Mr..."

"Randal." He offered her a squARe of purple paper.

Trudy realised with horror that this must be part of his reality and that just as at a party, realities could interlink. So that was why he'd been so tolerant of her recently. He'd found out her secret and joined in but it hadn't impinged on her own reality until now...

"What about your wife?"

"No need to worry about her," he said, "she's easily taken care of." He waved the sheet of squares. "You can have anything you want you know, Trudy," he said reaching for her hand. "Anything."

Marrying the boss mightn't be so bad. He was very rich. But he was also middle-aged and bald. If only he looked like Juan. Trudy took a squARe. Perhaps she'd just never noticed what a very attractive man Randal was.
"Anything?"

He signalled to a waitress. "Dessert."

"You don't have time for dessert, darlings!"

Randal turned to see his wife. "Julia, what the devil are you doing here?"

Trudy recognised Julia from the photo he kept on his desk.

"Whose reality is this?" demanded Trudy. "I only came out for lunch. You two can't just go around hijacking other people's realities!"

"Why not, darling?" said Mrs. Handley. "You hijacked my husband."

"You can keep him," said Trudy.

"No. I think I prefer your waiter," said Julia. "Ready, Juan?"

Juan offered Julia his arm.

"Now, if you two will excuse us, we have an alternate reality to get on with. Adiós."

Trudy and Randal, crumpled with pain, reached for the sheet of squARes. If only they could change just one thing before it was too late to return to their own realities.

"Oh, I shouldn't bother, dears," said Julia. "The reality is, I poisoned everything!"

Devotion

by Clarissa Angus

Today, you're wearing the silk blue tie with the lavender butterflies floating across its middle.

I've always liked that tie on you. The blue is just deep enough to compliment your masculinity without overcompensating. The butterflies, no bigger than stamps, are subtle reminders of your sensitivity, how you'd give up your seat on the tube for an elderly person without thinking about it.

I'm running a little late today because I overslept. I arrive at our café and see you at the counter getting your cappuccino, probably with chocolate sprinkled on top. You eye the croissants, rolls and cupcakes pressing their faces against the glass of the delicatessen display. My eyes sweep themselves over your back. A little back fat has started to poke out of your suit. I do like a little junk in my man's trunk, but not too much.

You choose a piece of shortbread just as you catch sight of a table, make a beeline for it after paying. In your hurry to save us a seat, you don't see me, but that's OK.

I'm forced to wait a little longer for my skinny latte because my barista is clearly new and therefore useless.

He apologises for the delay and asks me to take a complimentary pastry or cake. I shoot a quick look your way and see that you've already demolished the shortbread.

You stare out of the window into the rain while your hands distractedly cradle a book. I love that about you: that you still read books while everyone else around you hold their smartphones or tablets.

Those hands. Out of nowhere, I start to fantasise. I meet you at your office after dark - with a picnic basket - having anticipated you'd have skipped lunch to meet deadlines. I wear nothing except expensive lingerie underneath my long winter coat. You're hungry, but it's a different kind of hunger when we meet, the kind that sees you rip open my coat as we fall to the floor in a crumpled mess.

The security guard who let me up will know what we're up to, but there are no cameras in the boss's office.

I choose a piece of shortbread and make my way to our table. I can't take my eyes off you as I approach. A warm flush floods through me – I'm overwhelmed by romance.

You look up at me as I draw near. Your lips twitch. Your eyes blink double time. Your mouth starts to stiffen in distress. I'm not a fan of that expression.

"Can I take this seat?" I ask.

You look around the café wildly before looking back at me. You try to speak but your voice catches itself on the back of your throat.

"Thanks," I say. "Would you like this piece of shortbread? I got it on the house because my order was delayed by thirty seconds."

As I speak, you're packing up your things. I'll try to hide my disappointment. You stop briefly to stare me down with those big browns, the dim lighting of the café betraying flecks of fear. You lean over the table as close to me as you dare to get.

"You have to stop this," you hiss. "Otherwise, I'll call the police again."

I shrug, then laugh and push the shortbread across to you. "I'm not going to eat this."

You stand, tall, angry and as sexy as hell. Your eyes never leave mine as you storm out.

I hope I get to see you wear that tie again, soon.

A Matter of Taste

by Susan Howe

Guy leaned back in his chair, watching through narrowed eyes as the women moved round. His latest three-minute partner stood and stretched the scrap of skirt over her skinny rump. He brushed an imaginary fleck from his sleeve. She scowled and hurried away. It was less than a week until Christmas and stress darkened every face.

Guy shared their panic. He understood the urgency of finding someone to deflect questions from anxious parents, the mockery of siblings, the misery of another solitary New Year's Eve. And yet he despised them. Scratching around on the surface, their dreams lacked any trace of grandeur.

He tapped a manicured fingernail on the paper cloth as his next date swayed towards him. Rising slightly while she shuffled into place, Guy summed her up in the second it took to exchange names.

Gaunt and hollow-eyed, there was nothing real about her from the unlikely fan of lashes to the cold gleam of bleached teeth. Despair blocked his attempt at a smile long before it reached his lips. He sipped his drink and allowed her shrill chatter to wash over him.

Piped sleigh bells marked the end of his torture and he rose with a nod, intending to slip away. Head down, he risked a quick peek into the adjacent booth – and froze – afraid the flickering candlelight had deceived him. Holding his breath, he looked again.

Softly bulging flesh creased at elbow and wrist. Dimpled hands played with a lock of auburn hair. A gentle flight of chins flowed into a ripe, freckled bosom. Guy swallowed. This was more like it.

He held out his hand, trembling slightly as it closed on the warmth of hers.

"Guy."

"Paloma. But my friends call me Plum."

"Plum." He savoured the richness of the word. "How delightful."

***

He inspected his table, cloth in hand, ready to whisk away any blemish that marred its perfection. Reflected lights twinkled in antique crystal and silverware, solid against white damask. A sumptuous garland of cones, berries and fruit adorned the mantle. Flames leapt in the hearth and tempting aromas wafted through from the kitchen.

Guy glanced at the clock, hoping she would be ready on time. He needed to impress his father; to gain his approval at last. No more raised eyebrows, no more nostrils flared in contempt. Above all, no more doubts about his inheritance.

He studied himself in the mirror, shoulders back,

chin raised, grateful the gaudy SpeedFreak logo had caught his attention. *Satisfaction guaranteed or your money back.* It was going to be worth every penny.

***

Guy blinked away tears of joy and relief as the pressure of the hand on his shoulder increased. His father's eyes shone.

"She's a beauty, son. Congratulations."

They gazed at the face before them. Tiny beads of sweat glistened on Plum's brow, as though she understood the stakes and was straining to please. Raising his glass, Guy smiled, reached forwards, and plucked the apple from her mouth.

Differences

by John Ritchie

"What difference does it make?" Mike rolled onto his back and rubbed the place on his shoulder where Angelique had just bitten him.

"Just curious, that's all. I like to know as much about my victims as possible. If I am going to look them in the eyes before I kill them I like too know what I am going to see."

"Green. No, grey, Well, maybe, greyish green or greenish grey. Ah, what the hell, a couple of more days and she'll be crow-bait anyway."

"Well, aren't you the romantic?"

"What's biting your ass?" All this talk of his soon-to-be ex-wife was beginning to irritate him.

"You were, a little while ago, but..." she intercepted his hand, "I need to have a shower now, and then take care of some business."

Mike watched Angelique's slim, graceful figure negotiate the wreckage of their hotel bedroom on her way to the en-suite. She was really something; apparently, as cool as a glacier, but hot as a volcano between the sheets and when the one erupted through the other the collateral damage was something to see.

Angelique showered quickly and efficiently. As she twisted and turned under the hot water she thought about the pistol she had purchased for this hit. A little Russian piece: barely bigger than her hand.

The man in the gun-shop could barely contain his joy at getting rid of this piece of junk, though he tried to pretend that it was the ideal weapon for dealing with muggers and he was parting with a real gem.

Angelique had played dumb, pretending she didn't know anything about guns. Disguised in thick-framed glasses and cheap mis-matched clothes she hoped she looked like a librarian or something. Anything, other than what she really was.

When the man showed her the shells for the gun, she pretended to be shocked.

"Oh my, they are really small aren't they? Will they be big enough, you know, to make a man"... she blushed and simpered... stop."

The shopkeeper leered at her.

"Shoot 'em in the Family Jewels," he gestured at the baggy crotch of his trousers, "or shoot 'em in the head, either way they gonna lose interest, pretty fuckin' quick. To be honest lady, it don't make no difference. The bigger the bullet the bigger the hole, but at the end of the day it's where you shoot 'em that matters. Shoot 'em in their upstairs brains or shoot 'em in their downstairs brains or, heh, better still, shoot 'em in both. End of."

As she reached to turn off the shower, Angelique heard the bathroom door open.

"Gotta take leak."

"I'm finished in here if you want to wait."

She heard the seat of the toilet bang against the low-rise cistern, clearly he didn't want to wait.

Angelique turned her head to spray water in her ears. Mike may be doing what came naturally, but she didn't have to listen.

She gave it a minute and then turned off the water. Reaching up to the rack behind her, she pulled down a towel and wrapped it around herself. Then she reached up again and took the little Russian automatic from between the remaining towels.

When she stepped from the shower, Mike was naked, bent, over the washbasin cleaning his teeth. He saw her reflection in the mirror and was turning his head to say something when she jammed the muzzle of the pistol between his buttocks and pulled the trigger, twice. Mike dropped to his knees, his chin coming down hard on the edge of the washbasin, then he fell on his side, blood welling from between his fingers where they clutched the torn flesh of his groin.

He twisted round to look at her, confusion in his eyes.

"You hired me to kill your wife and her lover because you thought she was having an affair with one of your business partners. When your wife found out, she offered me double to kill you instead and spare her lover. What made the difference was that while you were right about the affair, you were wrong about the lover. Davis Jones isn't having an affair with your wife, I am."

One Door Closes...

by John Trevillian

Click.

The sound of the door closing – of the iron lock snapping into its aged steel keep – is the sweetest I've ever heard. I lean my sweat-drenched back against the freezing metal and breathe steam.

Mary, my wife of only three days stands beside me, her shock-white face etched in moonlight that creeps in through the single barred window. I can smell her amber perfume even now, even over the sting of oil and mildew. It reminds me of our first night in Reykjavik. John Dory and Sancerre at the 101 Hotel. The honeymoon suite, naturally.

How I blushed as I handed her the poem. How she read my words about her, and laughed at what love had made me do.

But that was all before the cross-wilderness trek east out to Skálafell. To the remote and frozen outpost. To this.

There's a resounding slam as something large hits the metal at my back. Making it jump. Making me jump.

Outside, the shrieks of the rabid undead or body snatchers or whatever the hell the packs of demonic shapes truly are diminish to growls. I glory that we've escaped – both of us – managed to get from the chaos and carnage at the ski lodge and find somewhere secure.

Whatever function this room has is lost in the shadows, but with only two solid doors and everything barred and braced, we are safe. Trapped and alone, yes, but safe.

"I thought I'd lost you," I say into the dark. "When I came back and you weren't in the cabin..."

"I'm fine," Mary replies in a voice that screams all shades of everything but fine.

I was out playing pool when the madness began, when the quiet of the bar room was shattered and the things rushed in. I soon learned how they only superficially looked like us, how when they attacked – a hideous process of attaching to people's mouths and regurgitating down their throats – the monsters' features dissolved like wax revealing some other form beneath. How afterwards the victims recovered and rose to become just like them. It's all too horrifying to take in.

With my eyes I check her over. Her auburn bob of hair, her stiff shoulders, the way her hands tremble as she forces them against her chest.

"Thank God, you're not one of them," I say, hugging her.

She returns the hug awkwardly, then withdraws, eager it seems to get away from the massing ghouls outside. It takes her only a few steps to reach the other side of the tiny room and the second entrance. But the creatures are swarming far quicker than her. Are already there, too.

"Check it's locked," I urge. And she does and it is. I cross to where my wife is waiting, there by the other door. She's still traumatised, her face solid and unsmiling. After this, I doubt she'll ever smile again. I take her hand, but she draws away. In the little light that remains her eyes are dead as stones at the bottom of the ocean.

The walls are alive with the clawing of the creatures, then the frosty window, and finally we hear them crawling over the corrugated roof. I imagine heaps of the snarling horrors covering the metal shed completely. Making it appear as if built of bodies. Writhing, gore-soaked bodies who poured out of the night and fed upon guests and guides and huskies alike. Then I imagine them getting inside and doing that to Mary.

"Don't worry, honey," I answer the thought in both our minds. "I won't let that happen. You're mine."

Then I reach out, but not to her.

"Sam," she says, panicking, "what are you doing? Honey, no– Not the door!"

As my mouth meets hers she realises, but it's too late. My face is already melting.

But it's OK, I think as the bile rises in my throat, because the poem's safe. I have written her down.

So now she will live forever.

With us.

Click.

Reunion
by Hank Johnson

"Ya know, son, I never was much of a father. Much a one, hell I wasn't one in your life at all the way it was."

The grizzled older fellow looked down at his coffee as he said the words. The backs of his bony hands were covered with sun spots, fingernails permanently stained from nicotine, and he smelled like an old ashtray.

The younger man smiled, nodded.

The older man continued, "But ya know, I knew I couldn't do right by ya, let alone yer Ma, so's I up an' left." He paused, then, "While she was still in county hospital, a few hours after you was born I left. Jus' too much. I mean, the both a ya and everything else, ta handle."

He stirred the coffee slowly in the stained white crockery mug.

"Never figured she'd give ya up. Proud of ya, she was. Doted on ya, she did. Least that's what I heard."

He stirred, head bent down toward the cup, a pate covered with thinning white curly hair in need of shampoo. A photo of a First Cav PFC holding an M16 wearing a flak jacket, him in earlier years, lay on the worn Formica surface between them.

"Drink. Dope. That shit can make even a Bible thump'n Baptist girl from Enid, Oklahoma, 'bandon. Left ya in the back a somebody's car I heard, cut out for parts unknown, California, tok'n, suck'n, sip'n and smok'n."

He prodded the photo toward the younger man.

"Address's on the back of the pitcher there. Figured ya might like the keepsake, my Nam photo I mean, an' I told ya I could get ya the address on the back." He hesitated, then said tentatively, "Son."

The younger man pulled the photo over the counter, nodded, put it into his breast pocket.

"Two years to find me, ya say. Me on the road so much. Betcha used one of those internet services, huh?" He looked up into the eyes of his son, "I'm more un glad ya did. This is almost like on Morey or Opry, like a reunion show."

The younger man smiled, nodded.

"Heard ya had some tough times with those foster folks they put ya in with after your ma dumped ya. Heard what that Vandevere bastard and his old lady were doin' ta ya. They never nailed them fer a thing. Retired, I hear, just back down the road in Phoenix, same trailer park off Bell Road."

They walked out to the old man's rig. The son, with father's encouragement, climbed up in the cab and looked around. It smelled like he did, like an old ashtray. He looked into the sleeping compartment behind the cab, and noted where the pillow was up against the outside bulkhead.

"Good rig for an old fart like me, huh? Times back then I never figured I'd have an outfit like this, let alone a good woman and two grown boys. Make that three, now my first one found me."

They shook hands among the idling diesel rigs parked for the night at the truck stop west of Phoenix. The father said he'd enjoyed the reunion, said he was going to get some sleep and said, "Look me up again soon."

Later the younger man walked casually between the clattering rigs until he came to his father's sleeping cab. He fired five shots through the side of the compartment where the pillow would be, where the old man's head would be. The popping of the pistol was lost among the racket of the idling diesel engines.

He walked brusquely back to his car thinking about the old man back in the rig and about the Vandeveres both lying dead in their trailer home in Phoenix. He remembered waking up there every morning as a kid, the smell of dirty diapers and sour milk, before the terrors began. He smiled to himself as he walked.

He looked at the address on the back of the photo, and figured he could be in Riverside by morning in time to visit his mother before breakfast.

Taking Care of Business

By Morgan Songi

Moonlight shadows lay under the trees below my office window when I pulled on my coat and forced myself out the door. I wasn't comfortable leaving after dark. I had to navigate three flights of stairs in order to get to the courtyard, and the concrete walls were slick and grimy with soot-like smudges of black. There was gray-green moss in the corners where the janitor's mop never reached and crud built up over time.

On my lunch break I'd overheard a conversation that troubled me. Ruby took a bite out of a tuna sandwich and said, "It stinks to high heaven."

I thought for a second she was referring to the fish.

"Did you know Steve's trying to sabotage Mike's promotion?" She shook a vinegar and salt chip at Amanda for emphasis and flushed bright red when she noticed I was standing behind her. "Mike, I didn't..." she stammered.

"Don't worry," I said. "There's never been any love lost between me and Steve. To tell you the truth, I'd like to kill him and tell God he died."

The three of us had a good laugh over that one.

Now, with the weekend ahead of me, I planned to devote my talents to taking care of Steve. He had a laundry list a yard long of nasty habits, but the absolute worst was the way he manhandled food. He gobbled like the world's greediest dog going face first into a bowl and the resulting noises were disgusting. Steve's greed was matched only by his sneakiness. Two minutes after the office manager filled the candy bowls he'd sidle past, grab several handfuls and shove them in his pockets. Then he'd ram a fist-full down his gullet. Without chewing. I knew I could use that.

But first I had to get down the stairs without imagining footsteps closing in behind me in the stairwell.

A guilty conscience? the nagging little voice in my head whispered.

"Not on your life," I said aloud.

Something scurried on the stairs below me.

Not even a little?

"No way."

I shut the voice off. "Steve is a gluttonous nasty piss-poor excuse for a human being and I'm going to enjoy putting him out of everybody's misery."

It was going to be easy. I have a set of rejects among the glass pieces I'd blown when I decided to exercise my crafty side. I started with glass beads, and when I got bored I turned my interest to miniatures. I was proud of my series of tiny bon-bons. They were amazingly realistic but there was a problem. An interaction between the chemicals and the colour chips caused the finished pieces to fracture into slivers of fine glass when the temperature reached ninety eight degrees Fahrenheit.

A failure I would soon turn into to a success. Greedy-gut Steve was going to end up with a belly full of glass before he had a chance to screw me over at the next managerial review.

Destiny, A Demise

by Mikey Jackson

Your name is Baxter. Male. Lost somewhere in your thirties. You've been watching her house for the last two hours. You're parked a sensible distance away. Smart move. Yet close enough to marvel at her dreamful silhouette every time she addresses the outside world through the shy gap between her bedroom curtains. Sly move. The black paintwork renders your car invisible in the moonless gloom of a chilly winter's evening. Ooh, you're good.

Heh, you've got a thing about congratulating yourself. It probably makes you look arrogant to others, but do you care? No. You're not here to make friends.

You're here to kill a girl.

You watch her latest trick leave the house. He wears the mother of all smiles. You know that smile well. You clock that same picture of overwhelming satisfaction in the mirror every time you leave her bedroom. You know what that smile means. She was amazing tonight. She's amazing every night.

Her name is Destiny. She is a goddess. Obsession makes you love the girl. That same obsession makes you hate the bitch. You have touched, tasted and feasted upon every square centimetre of her heavenly form, yet you know nothing about her. The downside is, she's aware of too many of your dirty little secrets. Word is she's planning to end your career with what she knows. This is why tonight she must bid farewell to this life.

Permanently.

You enter her home via the back door. No need to break in. Destiny gave you a key. She likes you, she trusts you, the girl thinks she knows you inside out. Huh, she certainly knows too much, that's for sure. But at the same time, she doesn't know enough.

As you ascend the stairs, you hear Destiny in the shower. She's a creature of habit. This is her protocol. She entertains, she blows their minds, she counts the banknotes, she waves goodbye, she washes their lust away. They come, they go, and in between, they spend a lot of money.

But not you. Mr Baxter always gets it for free.

You enter her bathroom. Destiny lobs across a broad smirk as she soaps herself inside that clear glass cubicle. It's as if she expected your company. And wanted it. Badly.

You peel off your garments. You clothe your tool with rubber. You can never be too careful. You know exactly where she's been.

You step inside the tiny, transparent cell. Cascades of water mount a relentless attack upon your bare skin as eager hands travel her hills and vales, from the smooth slenderness of her legs right up to the delicate softness of the neck you've kissed a thousand times before. Inside this girl, you are invincible, you are a king, you are everything you aspired to be. She is your heaven, your dreamland, your nirvana. You wish you could stay within her warmth forever.

But you can't. This paradise must end. Tonight.

The two of you cry out as your shared pleasure is finally spent. That's when you attack.

Destiny's lifeless body heads south. Sheets of water rain down upon her naked frame. Her eyes, glassy and unblinking. Her lips, slightly parted, as if preparing to speak.

You get dressed. You drive away. You arrive home. Time for another shower. All traces of Destiny, scrubbed away and lost forever down a gurgling plughole.

They say criminals should never return to the scene of the crime, but you have no choice.

You're also a policeman.

Upon arrival, you are greeted by a fresh-faced plod.

"D.S Baxter, I presume?"

That's your name, he'd better not wear it out. You don't quite catch his handle. PC Somethingorother.

"You'll find the victim upstairs," the uniform says.

As you amble into the bathroom, you lend poor

Destiny one final glance. You're sorry, you truly are, but it had to be done.

P.C Somethingorother asks, "Did you know this girl, sir?"

You tell him, "Destiny was one of my informants."

"Do you suspect foul play?"

You shake your head with monster doubt as you deliver your verdict. "Looks to me like she slipped in the shower and broke her neck. It's unfortunate. But accidents happen."

Biographies

Annie Evett is a prolific scribbler of characters, weaver of storylines, champion of the short story, professional cat herder, wielding a balanced editing razor whilst beating recalcitrant words into shape. She is a contributing editor in a number of publications and manages a small indie publishing house committed to promoting the short story form. She tweets @AnnieEvett.

Annie Mitchell wields a mean 6 HB pencil infusing her eclectic artwork with years of teaching, traversing the corporate landscape and motherhood. An emerging artist and photographer, she has had a number of brushpainting and sketches published. Check her tweets @AnniemMitchell or photos over at http://instagram.com/anniemmitchell.

Cathy Lennon lives and works in the north west of England. Her short fiction has been published in print and online and she has been shortlisted for several writing prizes. You can find her on twitter @clenpen.

Clarissa Angus is a Londoner raised by wonderful Jamaican-born parents. Sometimes, she gets lucky with her writing. If you're curious, find her on Ether Books and ABC Tales. She's been published in The Artillery of Words and *Litro* magazine, and was shortlisted for the Bridport Prize Short Story short list 2012.

CM Stewart writes speculative and experimental fiction because the voices tell her to. She also occasionally ends sentences with a preposition. She lives with her spouse and two cats in the northern United States.

Donna McLaughlin Schwender's work has appeared in Haunted Waters Press' From the Depths, Grey Wolfe Publishing's Legends, and Prompt and Circumstance's Promptly. For reasons unbeknownst to her, death has become the main theme for most of her writing. She's a little freaked out by that fact.

Hank Johnson is a mystery fiction writer with the proceeds of his published books also being donated to the Foundation for Blind Children.He races cars, writes and records music, cooks and develops recipes, enjoys wine, travel, creating art and does professional photography.

Jacqueline Pye has been writing non-fiction since her mid-teens, with topics that include child development, parenting, humour and psychology. She turned to writing short fiction, mainly dark – love, revenge, jealousy, psychosis and has recently published her first collection with some of the stories listed, commended or placed in competitions, and a number have appeared in other anthologies. She is currently working on her second collection.

J Adamthwaite lives in London and writes magical realism, although she enjoys different styles. She loves writing that explores the beauty in the mundane and finds the everyday detail we forget to see.

John Ritchie writes Flash Fiction because he hasn't got the imagination or the stamina to write anything longer. Indeed the strain of composing this biography means that he will probably have to go and have a lie down in a darkened room, when, if he ever, he actually gets finis...

John Trevillian is an English novelist, poet, shaman and award-winning author of three novels (The A-Men, The A-Men Return and Forever A-Men), plus writer of many other short stories, poetry collections and travel journals. He is also creator of the Talliston House & Gardens project, where he now lives. Find him on http://www.trevillian.com.

Kate Murray is studying at the University of Wales, Trinity Saint David. She's had a number of stories published; in the 2011 and 2012 anthology for Aberystwyth University, in the Five Stop Stories ebook Vol. 2, in the magazine 'Female First', and in The Lampeter Review.

Kenneth Crowther was born and raised in rural Queensland, Australia. He became interested in writing while working in media production, traveling the world making documentaries. As well as short stories and novels, he writes and directs independent films and stage plays and is currently studying a Master of Creative Writing.

Lance Manion is the author of five short story collections, the latest entitled "The Trembling Fist". He contributes to many online flash fiction sites and blogs daily on his eponymous website. He finds the 'na' at the end of banana as annoying as you would if it were bananana.

Margie Riley's been a bibliophile forever and knows that writing is a complicated game. She belongs to a book club (doesn't everybody?) and a writers' group. Margie's work has been published and she uses her status as an elder (not an old age pensioner or senior citizen please) to justify her gentle wielding of the editor's red pen. She likes Susan Howe's prancing idea.

Melissa Gutierrez holds an MFA in fiction from the University of Arizona. She lives in Northern California and works for an architecture and engineering firm. Find her on Twitter @mmgutz.

Mike Epifani is a product of a Syracuse, NY, upbringing. He currently lives in Chicago and obtained a degree in Creative Writing from Columbia College. He spends his time writing fiction and non-fiction for submission to various publications and does stand-up comedy routinely. More of his work and ways to contact him can be found at mikeepifani.com.

Mikey Jackson is a freelance writer, novelist and scriptwriter from the seaside town of Worthing, near Brighton, on the South Coast of England where the sun sometimes shines, but it mostly rains. Author of the novel Patience Is A Virgin, he writes scripts, novels, short stories, web copy, gags and letters to the milkman. More info at mikeyjackson.com.

Morgan Songi's nonfiction, short stories, personal essays and poetry have been published in literary journals in the US and Canada. She's a member of Willamette Writers, Oregon Writer's Colony, Word Association and WORDOS writing groups. She's an enrolled member of the Red Cliff Band of Chippewa in northern Wisconsin.

Oonah V Joslin is Managing Editor of Every Day Poets and she just loves writing short stuff.

Penegrin Shaw (Winner of the People's Choice Award and member of the *Talliston Writers' Circle*) is writing his first novel *Earthlight*, an alt world/sci-fi piece about a boy who lives on the moon with his father in the 1950's. He is also writing a shared world novel with three other authors called *Project Aspire* (available on Wattpad) and has a blog on Wordpress called *The Ribcage.* Tweet him @Penegrinshaw.

Susan Howe's short stories have won several prizes and been widely published over the last few years. 'The Beast Next Door', has also been produced as a short independent feature film: http://www.buggerofakid.com/the-beast-next-door.html. She is looking forward to prancing down the red carpet dripping with diamonds and designer gear.

CPSIA information can be obtained
at www.ICGtesting.com
Printed in the USA
LVOW12s0135240316
480522LV00002B/20/P

9 780987 533197